How Pap

MW01256572

Contents

written by Julie Ellis

1

Most paper is made from large, quick-growing softwood trees, like pines. The trees are specially grown for papermaking. Millions of new trees are planted every year so that there will always be new trees growing. When the trees are cut down, their branches are cut off to make logs.

pine trees

It is not easy to drive large trucks close enough to pick up the logs. Sometimes logs are floated down a river because that is an easier way to move them.

4

floating logs

Once the logs reach the timber mill, the bark is taken off. They are chopped into small wood chips, which are then taken by truck to a paper mill.

wood chips

The chips are turned into wood fiber by grinding them between two strong discs. Old paper can also be used for fiber. The wood fiber is turned into pulp by adding steam.

The pulp is washed and strained to take out any large bits of fiber. Water is added to make the pulp liquid. Sometimes bleach is used to make it white, or color can be added.

The pulp is then pressed onto a wire screen. It looks like paper, but it is very wet. The wet paper is sent through rollers to squeeze the water out. When the paper has been dried, it goes through more rollers to make it smooth.

paper rolls

There are many different kinds of paper that need to be finished in different ways. What will the paper be used for? Most paper needs a special finish sprayed onto both sides. Some paper needs to be soft, and some needs a smooth, shiny finish.

The paper is put on a large roll so it can be cut, wrapped, and labeled. It is loaded onto trucks and taken to stores to be sold. Paper is not all used for writing. How many different uses for paper do you know?

Look around the room to see where paper is used. How do you use paper at home? Paper towels should be thick enough to hold water. Egg cartons are made from recycled paper. Cardboard boxes need to be strong to hold heavy things.

Newspapers can be poor quality paper, because they are read just once. Building paper is special heavy paper used in buildings. Good quality paper is used to make books like this one you are reading. Photo paper needs a special coating.

Every year, about half of all the paper used is recycled. This helps to get the most use out of every tree that is cut down. It also helps to keep paper out of landfills.

Unwanted paper can be made into useful new paper again. It can be used to make labels, packages, bags and tickets, as well as to send messages.

Paper can still be made by hand, as it was hundreds of years ago. It is easy to change the look of hand-made paper. You can add coloring or pieces of leaves, flower petals, or glitter to the pulp. Could you use your imagination and make your own special paper?